Children of the World

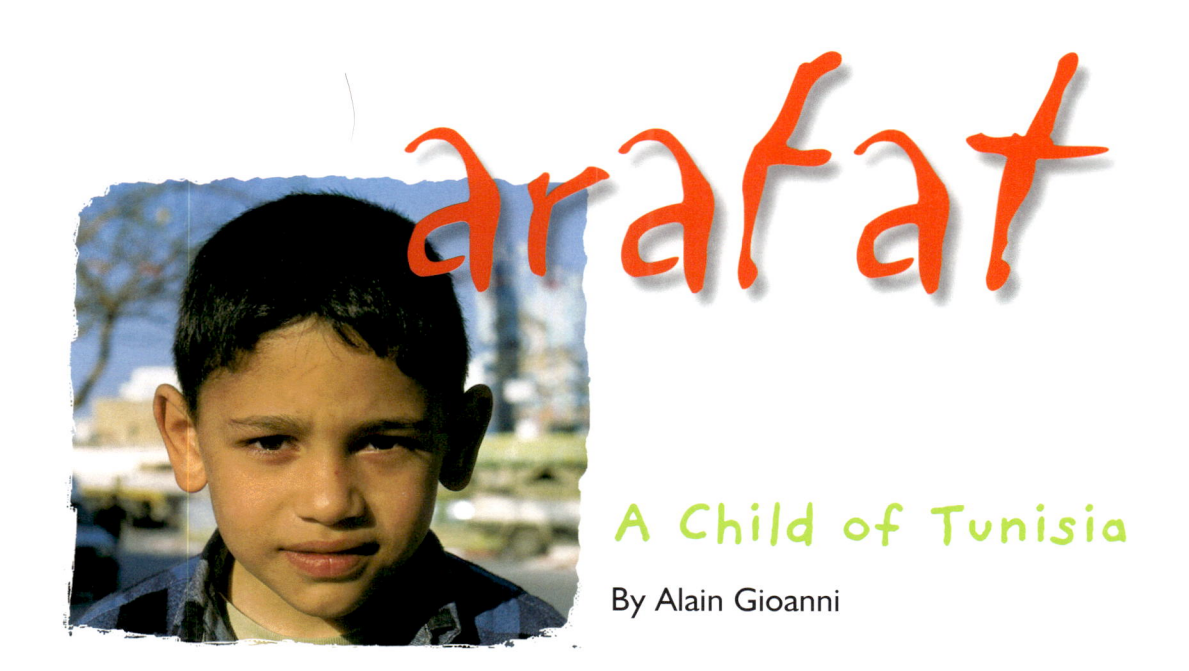

arafat

A Child of Tunisia

By Alain Gioanni

BLACKBIRCH PRESS
An imprint of Thomson Gale, a part of The Thomson Corporation

THOMSON
GALE

Detroit • New York • San Francisco • San Diego • New Haven, Conn. • Waterville, Maine • London • Munich

THOMSON
GALE

© Éditions PEMF, 2001

First published by PEMF in France as *Arafat, enfant de Tunisie*.

First published in North America in 2005 by Thomson Gale.

Thomson and Star Logo are trademarks and Gale and Blackbirch Press are registered trademarks used herein under license.

For more information, contact
Blackbirch Press
27500 Drake Rd.
Farmington Hills, MI 48331-3535
Or you can visit our Internet site at http://www.gale.com

ALL RIGHTS RESERVED.
No part of this work covered by the copyright hereon may be reproduced or used in any form or by any means—graphic, electronic, or mechanical, including photocopying, recording, taping, Web distribution or information storage retrieval systems—without the written permission of the publisher.

Every effort has been made to trace the owners of copyrighted material.

Photo Credits: All photos © Alain Gioanni except Table of Contents collage: EXPLORER/Boutin (upper left); François Goalec (upper middle and right); Muriel Nicolotti (bottom left); CIRIC/Michel Gauvry (bottom middle); CIRIC/Pascal Deloche (bottom right)

LIBRARY OF CONGRESS CATALOGING-IN-PUBLICATION DATA

Gioanni, Alain.
  Arafat : a child of Tunisia / by Alain Gioanni.
    p. cm. — (Children of the world)
  ISBN 1-4103-0289-X (hardcover : alk. paper)
  1. Tunisia—Juvenile literature. I. Title. II. Series: Children of the world (Blackbirch Press)

  DT245.G47 2005
  961.1'04—dc22

2005000694

Printed in the United States of America
10 9 8 7 6 5 4 3 2

Contents

Facts About Tunisia 5
Tunisia 6
Kelibia, Arafat's City 8
Arafat's Family 10
Dinner at Home 12
At School 14
The Date Palms 16
Work in Tunisia 18
Traditional Ways of Working 20
The Great South 22
Other Books in the Series 24

Tunisia
ARCTIC
OCEAN
PACIFIC
INDIAN
OCEAN
ATLANTIC
OCEAN
ICELAND
SWEDEN
FINLAND
NORWAY
RUSSIA
ESTONIA
LATVIA
LITHUANIA
DENMARK
IRELAND
U. K.
NETH.
BELARUS
GERMANY
POLAND
BELGIUM
LUX.
CZECH
SLOVAKIA
UKRAINE
AUSTRIA
HUNGARY
MOLDOVA
SWITZ.
SLOVENIA
CROATIA
ROMANIA
FRANCE
ITALY
MONTE
PORTUGAL
SPAIN
KAZAKHSTAN
MONGOLIA
UZBEKISTAN
KYRGYZSTAN
AZERBAIJAN
TURKMENISTAN
TAJIKISTAN
NORTH KOREA
SOUTH KOREA
JAPAN
CHINA
CYPRUS
SYRIA
LEBANON
ISRAEL
IRAQ
IRAN
AFGHANISTAN
MOROCCO
JORDAN
Canary Islands
ALGERIA
LIBYA
EGYPT
KUWAIT
PAKISTAN
NEPAL
BHUTAN
WESTERN SAHARA
SAUDI ARABIA
QATAR
U. A. E.
OMAN
INDIA
TAIWAN
MYANMAR
BANGLADESH
LAOS
MAURITANIA
MALI
NIGER
CHAD
SUDAN
ERITREA
YEMEN
THAILAND
VIETNAM
CAMBODIA
PHILIPPINES
GAMBIA
GUINEA BISSAU
GUINEA
BURKINA
BENIN
NIGERIA
DJIBOUTI
SOMALIA
SIERRA LEONE
IVORY COAST
TOGO
GHANA
CENTRAL AFRICAN REPUBLIC
ETHIOPIA
SRI LANKA
LIBERIA
CAMEROON
UGANDA
KENYA
BRUNEI
MALAYSIA
SINGAPORE
EQUATORIAL GUINEA
SAO TOME & PRINCIPE
GABON
CONGO
RWANDA
ZAIRE
BURUNDI
TANZANIA
INDONESIA
PAPUA NEW GUINEA
ANGOLA
ZAMBIA
MALAWI
FIJI
NAMIBIA
ZIMBABWE
BOTSWANA
MOZAMBIQUE
MADAGASCAR
NEW CALEDONIA
AUSTRALIA
SWAZILAND
SOUTH AFRICA
LESOTHO
NEW ZEALAND

Facts About Tunisia

Agriculture:	grains, grapes, olives, dates
Capital:	Tunis
Government:	presidential republic
Independence:	March 20, 1956 (it was a former French protectorate)
Industry:	oil, mining, tourism, textiles, footwear, cattle and sheep raising, fishing
Land Area:	63,170 square miles (164,000 square kilometers)
Languages:	Arabic (the official language), French, Berber
Money:	the Tunisian dinar
Natural Resources:	oil, phosphates, iron ore, lead, zinc, salt
Population:	9,832,000; about one-third are under fifteen years old
Religions:	Islam (98 percent), Christianity (1 percent), Judaism (1 percent)

Tunisia

Tunisia is a small country in North Africa. It has been occupied over the centuries by the Greeks, the Romans, the Vandals, the Arabs, the Turks, the Italians, and the French.

The French made it a colony. Tunisia became an independent nation in 1956.

The Tunisian city of Monastir is a famous beach resort.

Goldsmiths have shops in the medina of Tunis.

The dunes of the Sahara are located in the south.

Tunisia's capital, Tunis, is a modern city of 1,600,000 inhabitants. The ancient area of Tunis, the medina, has been carefully preserved.

The eastern edge of the country is bathed by the Mediterranean Sea. There are several beach resorts here. The south is covered by the Sahara Desert.

A modern street in Tunis, the Avenue Mohamed V.

Kelibia, Arafat's City

Seven-year-old Arafat lives in Kelibia. This city is in northern Tunisia, at the tip of Cape Bon.

Right: Arafat and his sister, Mona.

Below: The city of Kelibia is seen from its fortress.

Above: A street of shops in Kelibia.

Right: Cape Bon is a peninsula located about 87 miles (140 kilometers) from Sicily.

Kelibia is an active fishing port and a pleasant city for tourists.

Arafat's Family

Arafat lives with his parents, his brothers and sisters, and his grandmother. His parents own a stationery store and bookstore.

Above: The Arafat family's stationery and bookstore is a busy place.

Left: Arafat helps a customer.

When Arafat is not at school, he helps his father in the store. He enjoys helping the customers, who are usually schoolchildren like himself or high-school students.

Arafat enjoys helping in his family's store.

Dinner at Home

Arafat watches his mother and grandmother prepare the meal.

Arafat's mother has just finished shelling the beans that she will cook.

Arafat really enjoys the couscous they make!

Arafat's mother prepares the vegetables for couscous, a traditional Tunisian dish.

13

At School

Arafat and his sister, Mona, go to one of the elementary schools in Kelibia. He is in second grade.

The school's schedule changes every day. One day class is from 7:30 to 10:00 A.M. and from 1:30 to 3:00 P.M. Another day, school is open from 10:00 A.M. to 12:30 P.M. Because there are so many students, this allows them to share the classroom.

The entrance to the Ali-Belhouene school.

Every morning, the students watch the Tunisian flag being raised in the courtyard of the school. They also listen to their national anthem.

Lessons are taught in Arabic, which is written from right to left. Later, some lessons will be taught in French.

Children salute the flag.

Above: Arafat has copied the number written by his teacher.

The date is written on the blackboard. Today is Wednesday, April 18, 2001.

The Date Palms

Tunisia is a farming country. All kinds of vegetables and fruit trees are grown there.

The tree that best represents the country is the date palm. The date palm is found everywhere, even in the desert.

In an oasis, crops are grown in the shade of the palms.

A fellah, or farmer, transports the vegetables he grew in an oasis.

Date palms grow in oases, and grains and vegetables grow in their shade.

Every part of the date palm is used. The trunk is cut into long beams and the branches are used for fires or fences. Most important, the sweet fruit, which keeps for a long time, is eaten. A full-grown date palm produces 264 pounds (120 kilograms) of dates a year.

Above: At the market, dates are sold side by side with olives and spices.

Right: Selling dates at the market.

A fisherman fishes in the port of Byzerte.

Work in Tunisia

Farming, fishing, and handicrafts are important activities in Tunisia.

Above: A shop displays local handicrafts.

Left: Local crops are sold at the outdoor market.

19

Traditional Ways of Working

Even though machines have replaced animals, some people still work as they did in old times.

Inset: Women transport water on donkeys.

Below: A Berber shepherdess tends to her flock.

Above: A farmer cultivates his field of chickpeas.

Right: Weavers make chechias, or headgear, that is worn by everyone.

The Great South

The Sahara Desert covers much of southern Tunisia. Bedouins live there. They spend part of the year in tents made of woven wool.

Their camels are the only animals capable of surviving the harsh desert.

Above: Setting up a camp.

Left: A traditional Bedouin tent is made of wool.

Once they find a place to camp near a well, families and their animals will stay for a few months. They will leave once the pastures are used up.

Many tourists come to explore the desert. They travel either on camelback or in an SUV.

Above: The camels wait for tourists in the windblown sand.

Couscous cooks over an open fire.

Below: The camels quench their thirst at the nearest well.

Other Books in the Series

Asha: A Child of the Himalayas
Avinesh: A Child of the Ganges
Ballel: A Child of Senegal
Basha: A Hmong Child
Frederico: A Child of Brazil
Ituko: An Inuit Child

Kradji: A Child of Cambodia
Kuntai: A Masai Child
Leila: A Tuareg Child
Madhi: A Child of Egypt
Thanassis: A Child of Greece
Tomasino: A Child of Peru